Funny Business

by

Steve Barlow

and

Steve Skidmore

First published in 2006 in Great Britain by
Barrington Stoke Ltd
www.barringtonstoke.co.uk

ISBN-10: 1-842993-74-7
ISBN-13: 978-1-84299-374-3

Printed in Great Britain by Bell & Bain Ltd

Find out more about Steve Barlow
and Steve Skidmore at:
www.the2steves.net

Contents

Chapter 1
A Good Idea?

"A man walks into a bar. Ouch! It was an iron bar!"

Des gave us a big grin. Liz just stared at him.

"See?" he said. "You think I mean a bar in a pub, then it turns out I'm talking about a steel bar. The man bangs his head. *Ouch!* Get it?" Des turned to me. "Ben thinks it's funny. Right, Ben?"

I shook my head. "Sorry, Des."

"OK, OK, let's try another one. I've got a million of them. A man won a trip to China – now he's trying to win one back." Des grinned.

I rolled my eyes, and my head too. "That's terrible," I said.

"Get it? He's trying to win one back," said Des. "Because he's stuck there, you see? He only won a trip *to* China. Not a return trip ..."

Liz shook her head. "If you have to explain a joke, it isn't a joke."

"Yeah?" Des was getting fed up. "Well, I wouldn't have to explain the joke if you weren't too stupid to understand it."

Liz was annoyed now. "I'm not stupid. And nor is Ben."

Des held up his hands. "OK, OK," he said quickly. "Sorry. No offence. Listen, don't worry, I've got a million of them. What about this one? A sandwich walks into a bar. The barman says, 'Sorry, we don't serve food here'."

Des burst out laughing.

I groaned. A lot. "That's even worse," I said.

Des stopped laughing. "You don't like that one either? Boy, you two are a tough audience."

"Des," I said, "these are kids' jokes. I need jokes that people *our* age will think are funny."

Des frowned. "What?"

"Ben needs jokes that teenagers and adults will like," Liz told him. "For the gig he's doing."

Was this such a good idea? I thought.

I'd booked myself into a slot in next Saturday's "First Timers" open night at *Chuckles Comedy Club*. I'd always wanted to be a comedian, and make people laugh. So I thought I'd have a go.

When I told Liz what I'd done, she said, "You?" and gave me one of her 'big sister' looks.

I said, "Yes, why not?"

She said, "What do you want to be a comedian for?"

I said, "So I can be rich and famous and get lots of girls."

She gave me another of her looks.

But it was already Tuesday. I only had four days to get ready, and I needed some good jokes to win the £50 prize for best comic of the evening. I asked Des to help out because he's always telling jokes at college. There's always a crowd round him, laughing their heads off. But it wasn't going well. For one thing, Liz and Des weren't getting on at all.

"I don't believe this," said Des in a hurt voice. "I'm giving up my free time for you. I don't have to be sitting here after college in this canteen with you two. I could be doing lots of other things. I've got loads of course work I need to finish …"

The idea of Des doing course work was a bit of a laugh in itself – but he was right. I had asked him for help and now Liz and I were telling him his jokes were no good. I began to feel a bit guilty.

"Sorry," I said. "It's just that it's the first time I've done anything like this. I don't want people to laugh at me."

"If you want to be a comedian," said Liz, "that's just what you *do* want."

"Hey, that's right!" I laughed. "Now *that* was funny!"

Des looked puzzled. "What's the joke? I swear I don't understand you sometimes. Do you want my help or not?"

"Yes, please," I said.

"Yes," said Liz in a tone of voice that meant "not really".

Des clapped his hands together – loudly. I rocked back in my chair. I wish he wouldn't clap so loud. "Here's a great one for you," he said. "You can start your act off with this one. How many blonde girls does it take to …?"

Liz held up her hand. "Hang on," she said. "Is this joke going to make out that blonde girls are stupid?"

Des thought for a second. "I suppose so…"

Oh no, I thought. *Wrong answer.*

"And what colour is my hair?" asked Liz.

Des looked at me. I looked away. *You got yourself into this one, mate*, I thought. *You get yourself out.*

Des took a deep breath. "It's erm ..."

"Blonde," said Liz. "And so is Ben's. And ... so is yours."

"Er, yeah, right," stuttered Des. "But me and Ben aren't girls ..."

Liz looked hard at him. "So, it's just blonde *girls* who are stupid? So, now you're being sexist. And just because a girl is blonde, why does it make her thick?"

"Because the bleach has washed her brains away!" Des's mouth snapped shut. "Sorry, I couldn't resist it," he said. "You give me a feed-line, out comes a gag. I can't control it. It's like a reflex action."

I smiled grimly. I knew all about reflex actions that you can't control.

"What are *you* grinning about?" Liz asked me.

"I didn't say a thing." I gave her my 'sad-puppy' look. It never works on her. "Come on, Des," I said. "You must have *some* gags I can use."

"Gags. Right. I've got a million of them." But Des was starting to lose it.

Chapter 2
It's Not Funny

One of the canteen staff came round with a black bin bag. She started to clear the crisp packets off our table. She pointed at my coffee cup. "Has he finished with that?"

Liz looked at her. "Why don't you ask him?"

The woman said nothing. She took the cup and wiped the table down with a wet cloth. Then she went away.

Des had been thinking. You could almost see the cogs turning in his brain as he looked for a joke that would be OK with Liz. "Right ... There was this Irishman ..."

"Racist! Next," Liz said.

Des put his hands out. "Aw, give it a try. It's funny ..."

"Next!"

"I suppose you don't want to hear about the gay bloke ..."

Liz stared at him. Her lips were tightly shut.

"I thought not." Des was starting to sweat. "OK. Not sexist, not racist? Er ... Oh yeah, here's a real funny one. Have you heard about the dyslexic who walks into a bra?" He waited for the laugh. There wasn't going to be one.

"Are you dyslexic?" asked Liz.

Des shook his head.

"Do you know anyone who is dyslexic? A friend? Anyone in your family?"

"Er ... no," Des said at last.

"So you don't know how it feels to be dyslexic?"

Des just shook his head again.

"Right. So why is making jokes about someone who has a problem funny?"

"Its just a laugh," said Des. "It's a play on words. Look, lighten up, okay? I mean, sure, some people might think some of my gags are a bit – you know – "

"Offensive?" said Liz.

"Well – yeah, if you like – but that's just too bad. I mean, if you're always trying not to hurt anyone's feelings, you'd never tell any jokes at all."

"What do you mean?" I asked him.

"I'm saying a joke is a joke, it's not personal. And if people can't take a joke, that's their problem. Some people have no sense of humour."

"Know any good jokes about people in wheelchairs?" asked Liz.

"Oh, yeah." Des saw me staring at him. "Er, no."

"I don't want to tell jokes like that, Des," I said.

Des looked at Liz. She said, "Not that sort of joke. All right?"

"But my jokes are funny," said Des. "People laugh."

"Some people," said Liz. "The stupid ones."

Des was stung into attack. "You don't understand humour. These are classics. Everyone finds them funny."

"We don't," I said.

Liz nodded. "You can say that again."

"We don't," I repeated.

Liz laughed and winked. "Face it, Des," she said. "You're about as funny as tooth-ache."

That's when Des lost it. Big time. "Right!" he shouted. "You think you're so clever – see how you like this. I'm going to enter the competition at the Comedy Club as well. My jokes against his. It'll knock the smiles off your faces when I win the 50 quid. You won't be laughing then!"

"We won't be laughing at your jokes," said Liz. "That's for sure."

"Oh, you're so funny," snarled Des. He picked up his coat and stormed out of the canteen.

Liz just sat there, looking at me.

"All right, all right!" I said. "I shouldn't have asked Des."

"Oh, he's harmless," said Liz. "He's just such a *bloke*."

15

I grinned at her. "Hey, what do you call a bloke with half a brain?"

Liz gave a shrug.

"Gifted!"

She laughed. "And what do you call a bloke with a big mouth and no brain at all?"

We both shouted the answer out. "Des!"

Chapter 3
Comedy Greats

We left college and went to wait for the bus. It was raining.

Some of the football lads on the sports course passed by. They're on United's books, so they reckon they're God's gift, the best around. One of them winked at his mates and yelled to me, "Hey, Killer! Fancy a game of footy then?"

Liz shouted right back at him. "When are they going to teach you to think and chew gum at the same time?"

The lad scowled at Liz. "You've got a smart mouth," he said. "What are you doing with that loser?"

"He's my brother," Liz said.

The lad said, "Oh – right," and looked away. That's when he saw his mates had gone on without him. "Hey! Wait up!" he shouted at them. They didn't slow down. He had to run to catch up.

I said, "I can look after myself you know."

Liz tried to smile but her face was sort of sad. "Of course you can."

That sort of thing happens sometimes. I try not to let it bother me. I like college most of the time. It's better than school. The teachers don't treat you like a kid. They let you call them by their first names and they don't talk down to you. And most of the people there are OK. Sometimes people say or do things that upset me, but not often on purpose. They just don't think.

Another good thing about college is that there aren't as many lessons. I used to hate the school time-table. Sometimes I had seven lessons a day. I spent most of my time just getting from one place to another, and I was late for almost everything.

Liz looked at the time-table. "There isn't a bus for 20 minutes. Shall we go and wait in the café across the road?"

"No," I said. "Too many steps up to it. Anyway, there's not enough room round the tables. I hate being blocked in."

Liz shrugged. "OK – how about going over to the supermarket for a bit?"

I didn't really want to go to the supermarket, but it was raining hard, so I said OK.

We crossed the road. I nearly slipped as I went down off the kerb, but luckily Liz was there.

We went into the supermarket. Liz went off to buy some girlie stuff, and I had a look at the DVDs.

When she came back, I said, "Hey, how about getting a DVD? That one looks good."

"Which one?" Liz asked.

"Look – third shelf down, four along – *Comedy Greats.*"

Liz picked it up. "Do you think this might give you some ideas?"

"It's worth a try."

"OK, let's buy it."

When we got home, Mum was lying on the sofa. The TV was on but she wasn't really watching it.

We said "hi". Liz put the DVD on the table.

"Is Dad out?" she asked.

Mum nodded. "He's working tonight."

Dad's a fireman, but he does other jobs when he's finished his shift. Mum's a nurse. She works shifts, too. It brings in the money to help pay for Liz and me to go to college. But all their work means we don't see much of them.

Liz said, "I'll make some tea." She went into the kitchen to put the kettle on.

"No tea for me, thanks," called Mum. "Did you have a good day at college?" she asked me.

"All right," I said. "I've got a lot of work to finish."

"I can't give you a hand tonight, sorry – I've got a meeting."

"No worries," I said.

"Are you and Liz OK to look after yourselves on Saturday? Dad and I are working."

"That's OK." I hadn't told Mum and Dad about the comedy club. They'd try to stop me if they knew. They try to protect me too much. I reckon the truth is Mum and Dad think I can't do a lot. They don't want me to be hurt or let down.

Mum picked up the DVD. "What's this? *Comedy Greats*?"

"I felt like a laugh tonight," I said.

Mum looked at the names of the comedians on the DVD cover. She pointed at one of them. "I thought he was dead!"

Liz had brought the tea in. She checked the name. "He *is* dead."

"I thought I hadn't seen him on telly for a while," said Mum. "I suppose I'd better get going now." She got up off the sofa. "Be good," she said and went out. We heard the front door close.

Liz put the DVD on.

Chapter 4
Life is Funny

There were lots of comedians on the DVD. The first one told some jokes. Then he went into a tap dancing routine.

"Call me chicken," I said, "but I don't think I'll be doing that."

Liz gave me a look. "I shouldn't sing either, if I were you."

"What's wrong with my singing?"

"You sound like a cow giving birth."

"Thank you for that." But I had to admit, she was right.

The next guy did impressions. He made fun of famous people. Liz laughed quite a lot. "Don't you think he's funny?" she asked me.

"I don't know," I said. "He's a bit cruel."

Liz shrugged. "Maybe. But the people he's making fun of wanted to be famous. No-one made them go into politics or get on TV. It was their choice."

I could see what she meant. We'd done some stuff about court jesters in History. A few hundred years ago kings had jesters. The jesters' job was to say things that no-one else could. They did this so the king wouldn't forget that he was only human.

Then there was a comic Liz and I didn't like. He wore a dinner jacket and a bow tie. He had a loud voice and said, "'Ere!" a lot.

I didn't like his jokes. He did the sort of gags Des wanted me to do. Now, I may not be a genius, but even I know that people from Pakistan are called Pakistanis, not what he called them. And when he started telling jokes about "cripples"...

Liz pretended to throw up. Then she used the remote control to fast forward through the rest of his act. "OK?" she said.

I nodded. "If all I can think of is jokes that make people feel bad about themselves, I won't bother turning up on Saturday."

The next guy was funny. He did a magic act, only everything kept going wrong. The more things went wrong, the harder he tried to put it right and the funnier it was.

Liz stopped the DVD for a moment. "Why are you laughing so much?" she asked.

"He's funny!"

"Yes, but *why*?"

I thought about this. "Because he's making fun of himself, not someone else."

Liz nodded, and pressed 'Play'.

The last comedian had us both in stitches. He didn't really tell jokes. He just talked about himself. About what it was like when he was a kid, growing up in a small town. The sort of things his mum and dad used to say. "Take that look off your face –

you'll stick like it!" and "Take your coat off inside or you won't get the benefit." Liz and I laughed. Our gran says that.

"I never understood our mum," he said. "Whenever I went out she'd say, 'Have you got clean underpants on?' and I'd say, 'What for?' and she'd say, 'In case you get run over.'" He looked puzzled. "What happens at the hospital if I'm run over?" He did a 'doctor' voice. "'That car really smashed you up, son. Can you feel your legs?' – 'Never mind my legs,' I say. 'Give it to me straight, Doc. Are my underpants clean?'"

We watched his act three times.

Liz cooked sausages for supper – my favourite. When we'd finished she cleaned up my jumper (I've always been a messy eater).

"I thought being a comedian was all about telling jokes," I said, "but it's not just that, is it?"

"What do you mean?" Liz looked at me.

"Well, telling jokes is part of it," I said, "and playing the fool, too. But I reckon what good comedians do is take something ordinary, and make you think about it in a new way. They say, 'Hey, this is funny. People are funny. Life is funny. It's okay to laugh.'"

"I suppose so," Liz said.

"So, if I want to be a comic, my jokes have to be about me. My life. I have to tell the truth, about what it's like to be me. Even if it hurts."

Liz nodded slowly.

I went on. "Because what a good comedian is really saying is, 'I'm laughing at myself, so you can laugh at yourselves. We live in a crazy world. We all do crazy things. It doesn't matter. Enjoy it.'"

That was a lot of words for me. I don't often go on like that. Liz was staring at me. Then she said, "Did you just work all that out yourself?"

I said, "Well, I'm not just a pretty face, you know."

She threw a cushion at me.

"Stop messing about," I said. "I'm getting some ideas here. I know what I'm going to do on Saturday. Grab a pen and write this down ..."

Chapter 5
The Big Test

Liz and I spent the rest of the week working on my act. It was hard work at first. I found it difficult to get the timing right and sometimes I forgot the order of the gags. But with practice I got better. By Saturday night, I thought I might even have a chance of winning the 50 quid.

When Liz and I arrived at *Chuckles*, the men on the door looked puzzled.

"This is Ben. He's in the competition tonight," said Liz. "He's got a slot on stage later on."

The two men gave each other a look. They shrugged, stepped back and let us in.

It was dark and crowded inside the club. At the far end of the room was the stage. It was lit by a couple of spot-lights. Some people sat on benches waiting for the comedy to begin. Others stood around chatting. Liz made sure I was OK. Then she went to find the manager and let her know we'd arrived.

Someone tapped me on the back. I looked up. It was Des.

"You turned up then?" he said. "Got any gags?"

"A few."

"I've got a million of them," said Des.

"So you told me."

There was a blast of music and the lights went dim. The host for the evening jumped onto the stage. "Good evening *Chuckles*!"

"May the best man win," I hissed at Des.

"Don't worry, I will," said Des. He moved off.

Liz came back. "What did Des want?" she asked.

"Oh, he was just wishing me all the best!"

On stage, the host was getting the audience in the mood. "So we've got 50 quid to give to the best 'first time' comic. Let's get on with it. Don't forget to laugh for our first act. Johnny Cook!"

The next hour was amazing. The room was like a bear pit. People laughed and jeered. If they didn't like the jokes they let the comic know. Most of the acts weren't much older than me. Some were good. Some were awful and didn't get any laughs at all. The comics who got the most laughs were the ones who told jokes about themselves. That was a good sign, I thought.

"You sure you're OK with this?" asked Liz.

"Oh yeah!"

Finally we got to the last two acts. Des and me.

"Right!" said the host. "He says he's got a million gags. Let's hope some of them are funny! Let's hear it for Des Bell!"

Des leapt onto the stage. "All right?" he shouted. "Good evening *Chuckles*!"

"Get on with it, you wally!" shouted a bloke in the crowd.

Des looked a bit worried. He took a deep breath and began. "Hey, guys. Here's one for you. How do you keep a woman happy?"

Uh oh! Bad joke alert, I thought.

Des gave the punch line. "Who cares?"

One or two blokes in the crowd laughed. The girls booed loudly.

"Sexist!" shouted Liz. I stared at her. "Well, he is." Then she began to boo as well.

And poor Des's act got even worse.

Racist jokes, sexist jokes, Des did have a million of them. And they were all bad. Des was in trouble. He was sweating buckets. His jokes were getting more and more jeers. He was desperate. To try and make things better he told a load of dumb blonde jokes. Bad move. The crowd booed and booed.

Liz bent down and whispered in my ear. "Why are all dumb blonde jokes so short?"

I shrugged.

"So that people like Des can remember them!"

"Nice one. You should be on stage."

"I'm going to be soon," she said.

Finally, the host came back onto the stage to help Des out. He grabbed the mike and pushed him off the stage. "OK. Thanks, Des. Don't give up the day job. Don't call us and we won't call you."

He turned back to the audience. "Now for our last slot tonight. Give it up for a young local lad. He's an act with a difference."

I took a deep breath. This was it. I gave Liz a smile.

"Go and kill them!" she said.

"That's a bit drastic," I joked. "I'll stick to making them laugh."

"Here he is!" shouted the host. "Let's hear it for Ben Smith!"

I made my way through the crowd as people clapped and cheered. I got to the stage and stopped.

I'd been so nervous, I hadn't noticed before. There was no ramp to get onto the stage. Just steps.

How was I going to get up there in my wheelchair?

Chapter 6
Ski-jumping

In the end, two blokes came up to the front. They lifted my chair and dumped me in the middle of the stage. No one was clapping now. People were looking at each other.

I could tell what they were thinking. How's this guy in a wheelchair going to be funny? He's got cerebral palsy. That's not funny. Wheelchairs aren't funny. We won't understand what he says. Speech problems aren't funny.

Well, I am going to be funny, I thought. *Like it or not.*

I looked at the mike. It was set up for someone to stand behind it. It was way above my head. I looked around for some help. I jerked my head, I said, "Oy." There were a few nervous giggles from the people in front of the stage. Liz came up on stage. She got the mike and fixed it down to my level. A few people clapped.

The spot-lights were set way above my head, too. I said, "What about some light?"

"Light?" said Liz. She pretended to look puzzled. Then she took a pen torch out of her pocket. She turned it on and shone it in my face. "Thanks a bunch," I said. There were more laughs.

Liz had got another mike. I turned to the audience. "Good evening," I said, "my name's Ben and here's my first gag. What do you call a guy like me, a guy with cerebral palsy, sitting in a wheelchair?"

Liz repeated what I'd said. Dead silence.

I said, "Call him what you like. What's he gonna do?"

Liz repeated this and I did the best I could to shrug. There were gasps and one or two people laughed again. Liz gave me a worried look. People were starting to feel awkward. It was the same old problem – when non-disabled people see someone like me, they don't see a person. They just see the disability.

42

I had to break the ice, fast. "Hey," I said, "if you don't like these jokes, don't blame me. It's the way she tells them."

Liz repeated this. It got a laugh.

I began to relax. *Get on with it,* I thought. Smile, speak clearly and don't drool too much. I moved into what Liz and I had worked on. She was going to repeat everything I said, then everyone would understand it.

"People ask me if I was born like this?" I waited a moment. Then I gave them the answer. "Of course not. I was a lot smaller!"

That got a big laugh.

"My mum says it took ages for me to be born," I went on. "The doctors got me out OK ... but the wheelchair took *forever.*"

There was more laughter and a couple of people clapped. The audience was settling and feeling more comfortable. So was I.

"I may not look quick in this chair," I said, "but I can move faster than anyone in this room."

There were some murmurs at the back. "No way," I heard someone say.

"It's true! I could nip out to the loo and be back here on stage so fast you wouldn't believe it."

I paused and waited. Comedy is in the timing.

"Do you want to see me do it again?"

The audience got it! Laughter filled the room.

I looked down and saw the United guy who'd had a go at me when Liz and I were at the bus stop. *Time to get my own back,* I thought. I winked at Liz. That was the signal for her to stop repeating my lines. This was one joke I wanted to tell on my own.

"Is there anyone in here from United tonight?" I asked, speaking as clearly as I could.

"Yeah!" The guy stood up and waved at the crowd.

"Well, I'm sorry if you can't understand me ... but I can't talk any slower!"

That gag brought the place down. Everyone was laughing now. The United guy had to take it in good spirit, but I could tell he wasn't happy.

"I went to the fun fair the other day. I had a go on the shooting range and won one of those big cuddly toys. Well, when I say *won* – they gave it to me, so that I'd put the gun down." I pretended I had a gun and I was shooting all over the place.

The roar of laughter made me jerk my head back. This was going well! I went on. Liz repeated some of the longer jokes. There's no point telling gags if your audience can't understand a word you're saying.

"I hate barbecues. At the last one we had, they asked me to toss the salad. So I did – right over the fence."

More laughs. I was really into my act now, talking about me and my life.

"I drool over girls. In fact I drool over most things ..."

I was laughing at the way the world sees me, and how other people react to disability.

"What's wrong with the way I talk? A BBC newsreader taught me to talk like this." I waited a moment. "The problem was he was drunk at the time."

More laughter. I was getting towards the end of my slot. I was loving it!

"I was going to finish with a tap dance. That's the one I do when I try to turn a tap on." I showed what happens when I try to turn on a tap. People who make taps don't think about people like me.

"Then I thought, no! I'll do something even better. So here comes the big finish!"

Liz spoke into her mike. "And now, for the first time anywhere, wheelchair impressions! Number one – water going down a plughole."

I ran my chair around in circles that got smaller and smaller until I ended up spinning round on the spot. This got a big laugh.

"And now – Scalextric!"

I ran my chair round in a figure of eight. People were crying with laughter.

"Buying cinema tickets!"

I ran my chair across the stage and back the other way, again and again. Just like you do at the cinema when there's nobody waiting to buy tickets but you still have to follow a zig-zag line and go around all those stupid tapes. Now I was right at the back of the stage.

"And last of all, The Ski-Jumper!"

I turned and raced my chair at the audience at top speed. There were squeals. Just as the front row was about to dive out of the way, I brought my chair screeching to a stop and said, "I'm Ben Smith. You've been a great audience. Thank you and goodnight!"

Everybody stood and cheered.

There were tears in Liz's eyes. I could see Des in the crowd. He looked a bit sick, but he was clapping too. He nodded at me and gave the thumbs up.

The host came on stage. He had five ten pound notes in his hand.

"Let's hear it for the winner!" He handed Liz the money.

"It's Ben's," she told him.

"Oh, yeah." The host looked puzzled for a moment. Then he tucked the money in my shirt pocket.

****

They've asked me back to do another comedy slot at *Chuckles*. This time, I get paid.

Who knows where this will all lead to? One thing I'm sure about – I don't want to be just another stand-up comedian. I want to be the world's best sit-down comedian.

They say comedy comes out of pain. If that's true, I'm never going to run out of jokes.

Gags? I've got a million of them.

Afterword

Steve Barlow used to work for a theatre company. One of the shows he did was with an actor called Alan, who had CP.

Alan was a very bright bloke. He had a degree from York University. But he was stuck in a wheelchair. He had very little control over his movements, and it was hard to understand him when he talked.

Steve's theatre company took their show to schools all over the country. Alan had an important part in the show. This was in the 1970s, when most kids with CP went to special schools. So the kids in a lot of the schools that Alan went to had never met anyone like him before. It was a big eye-opener for them to see someone with CP acting on a stage. They thought he was great.

Alan enjoyed it too. When the show first started going round schools, Alan insisted that he had a seat-belt on in his wheelchair all the time in case he fell out. As the tour went on, he started to leave the belt off more and more. By the end, he didn't put it on at all.

Steve Barlow thought about Alan when he was writing this story and thinking about Ben. Alan wasn't going to let CP or being in a wheelchair get the better of him. He was determined to beat the odds and make his dreams come true.

Barrington Stoke would like to thank all its readers for commenting on the manuscript before publication and in particular:

Alice Boardley

Alex Coy

Shaun Crate

Mrs A Curtis

Robbie Dee

Cait Evans

Bradley Farrington

Oliver Farrington

Oran Frostick

Tallon Grant

Luke Hazell

Sean Hill

Jessica Lewis

Matt Lloyd

Jessica Macready

Mrs Alwyn Martin

Alex Roche

Charlotte Scotland

Taylor Stevens

Olivia Wright

Become a Consultant!

Would you like to give us feedback on our titles before they are published? Contact us at the email address below – we'd love to hear from you!

info@barringtonstoke.co.uk
www.barringtonstoke.co.uk

Also by the same authors ...

The Doomsday Virus

Corder, Tim: Also known as Hack Jack. Has cracked the security systems of every secret service in the world.

Mission Objective: For Corder to destroy the Doomsday Virus.

Results of Failure: The end of the world

Chances of success: Not good ...

You can order *The Doomsday Virus* directly from our website at www.barringtonstoke.co.uk

Meet the Authors ...

Who is your favourite comedian?

SS Morecambe and Wise

SB Tommy Cooper

What's the funniest girl's/boy's name you can think of?

SS Skidmore is pretty funny

SB Thoda Pigbone (girl - honestly!)

What's the funniest word in the English language?

SS Bottom

SB Poo (judging by the reaction of kids whenever we say it)

What's your favourite comedy TV show?

SS M.A.S.H

SB Red Dwarf

What's the funniest thing that's ever happened to you?

SS Too embarassing to tell you …

SB Funny things only happen to other people – anything funny that happens to me is a tragedy

What makes you laugh/smile?

SS Life … (but it can also make you cry)

SB My friends

Who is the funniest person you know?

SS Steve Barlow

SB Steve Skidmore

What's the best joke you know? (no rude ones please!)

SS Q. What's pink and fluffy?
A. Pink fluff

SB Q. What's the difference between a buffalo and a bison?
A. You can't wash your face in a buffalo

Sticks and Stones
by Catherine MacPhail

Greg's sure he's the funniest and most popular guy in school.

So why does everybody think he's stolen Tony Harrison's mobile phone?

But it can't be a set-up. After all, everybody loves him ... don't they? He's going to need all his brains, and some help, to get him out of this one!

Diary of an (Un) teenager
by Pete Johnson

Sunday June 21st

"... I won't have anything to do with designer clothes, or girls, or body piercing, or any of it ... no, I shall let it pass me by. Do you know what I'm going to be? An (Un)teenager."

But then Spencer's mate Zac starts wearing baggy trousers and huge trainers. He buys himself a skateboard – and even starts going on dates with girls. But Spencer is determined:

"Dear Diary, I am going to stay EXACTLY as I am now. And that's a promise ..."

You can order *Diary of an (Un)teenager* directly from our website at www.barringtonstoke.co.uk

Exit Oz
by Catherine Forde

Meet the star of the show: Oz. My pet corn snake. 8 months old. 40cm long. About as thick as a ball-point pen.

So how can something SO small cause SO much hassle?

It happened like this: one minute Oz was there, in our hands, and the next ...? Well. He was gone.

Exit Oz.

How would we ever get him back?

You can order *Exit Oz* directly from our website at www.barringtonstoke.co.uk